Iris and Walter

and the Substitute Teacher

Iris and Walter

and the Substitute Teacher

WRITTEN BY

Elissa Haden Guest

ILLUSTRATED BY

Christine Davenier

Green Light Readers
Houghton Mifflin Harcourt
Boston   New York

For Liz Van Doren —E.H.G.

To Isabelle Davenier: the teacher all kids should have —C.D.

Text copyright © 2004 by Elissa Haden Guest
Illustrations copyright © 2004 by Christine Davenier

All rights reserved. Originally published in hardcover in
the United States by Harcourt Children's Books, an imprint of
Houghton Mifflin Harcourt Publishing Company, 2004.

Green Light Readers and its logo are trademarks of HMH Publishers LLC,
registered in the United States of America and/other countries.

For information about permission to reproduce selections from this book, write
to trade.Permissions@hmhco.com or to Permissions, Houghton Mifflin Harcourt
Publishing Company, 3 Park Avenue, 19th Floor, New York, New York 10016.

www.hmhco.com

First Green Light Readers edition, 2014

The text of this book is set in Fairfield Medium.
The display type was set in Elroy.
The illustrations were created in pen-and-ink on keacolor paper.

The Library of Congress has cataloged the hardcover edition as follows:
Guest, Elissa Haden.
Iris and Walter and the substitute teacher/written by Elissa Haden Guest;
illustrated by Christine Davenier.
p. cm.
Summary: When Iris's grandfather comes to her school as a substitute teacher,
she has a hard time sharing him with the other students.
[1. Teachers—Fiction. 2. Grandfathers—Fiction. 3. Jealousy—Fiction.
4. Schools—Fiction.]
I. Davenier, Christine, ill.
II. Title. PZ7.G9375Isl 2004
[E]—dc21 2003013524

ISBN:978-0-15-205013-9 hardcover
ISBN:978-0-544-22788-0 paperback

Manufactured in China
SCP 16 15 14 13 12 11 10 9

4500759493

Contents

1. A Surprise   7

2. The Special Helper   15

3. Misery   23

4. Ice Cream   37

1. A Surprise

Iris loved school.

She loved her sunny classroom.

She loved learning how to tell time.

She loved trading lunches with her
best friend, Walter.

And oh, how Iris loved Miss Cherry.

In the afternoons, when Iris and Grandpa
walked home from school, Iris told Grandpa
all about school and Miss Cherry.
And Grandpa told Iris stories
about when he had been a teacher.

One morning, when Iris arrived at school,
the principal was in the room.

"Did you hear the news?" asked Walter.

"What?" asked Iris.

"Miss Cherry is sick," said Benny.

"We're getting a substitute," said Walter.

"A substitute!" said Iris.

They had never had a substitute before.

Just then, the principal said,
"Good morning, boys and girls.
Today you are having a substitute teacher.

I am sure you will all listen to him
And be on your best behavior."
The door opened . . . and in came Grandpa!

2. The Special Helper

"Grandpa, what are you
doing here?" asked Iris.
"The regular substitute
could not come, so I'm
going to be the teacher
today," said Grandpa.
Iris was so excited.
Her grandpa was going to teach the class!
"Iris, why don't you be the special helper
today," said the principal.
"Oh boy!" said Iris.

Iris sat next to Grandpa while he told the class a wonderful story.

She erased the chalkboard after spelling.

Iris showed Grandpa where Miss Cherry kept the paint for art.

And at snack time, Iris and Walter passed out the apples.

When the bell rang, Iris said,

"Grandpa, that's the bell for recess."

"Oh no, it's raining," said Benny.

"Now we can't go outside," said Walter.

"Well then, it's the perfect day
for musical chairs," said Grandpa.
The children played one game
and then another.
"Your grandpa is so much fun," said Benny.
"He sure is," said Lulu.
Iris was so proud.

After school, the principal asked Grandpa
 if he could teach the class again the next day.
"Certainly," said Grandpa.
"Hooray!" said Walter.

On the way home,
Iris said,
"Grandpa, you're
a great teacher."
"And you, my girl,
are a great helper,"
said Grandpa.

"Guess what, Rosie?" said Iris that night.
"*I* was Grandpa's helper today. It was
so much fun! I can't wait for tomorrow."

3. Misery

The next morning, everyone was excited
to see Grandpa again.

"Are you going to tell us another story?"
asked Benny.

"This morning I'd like someone
to tell *me* a story," said Grandpa.

All the children raised their hands.

Iris was sure Grandpa was going to pick her.
But Grandpa picked Benny.

At snack time, Jenny asked Grandpa,
"May I pass out the crackers today?"
"Of course," said Grandpa.
But I'm the helper, thought Iris.

At lunch, Iris wanted to sit next to Grandpa.

But Grandpa never sat down.

He was too busy.

Benny needed a Band-Aid.
Lulu lost her sweater.
And Jenny had left her
lunch bag at home.

In the afternoon, Grandpa said,
"Let's go for a walk. Everyone can find
something interesting to give Miss Cherry
tomorrow."
Benny and Jenny rushed to hold
Grandpa's hands.
He's my grandpa, thought Iris.

"Iris, what are you going to give Miss Cherry?"
asked Walter.

"I don't know," said Iris.

"Do you want to give her this leaf?"
asked Walter.

"No," said Iris, and she walked away.

Back at school, Lulu said,
"Look at the rock I found."
"I found a leaf," said Walter.

"Iris, what did you find for Miss Cherry?"
asked Grandpa.

"Nothing!" said Iris.

"Why doesn't everyone make a card
for Miss Cherry," said Grandpa.
While everyone was drawing,
Grandpa went over to Iris.
"Iris, what's wrong?" he whispered.
"Everything," said Iris. "I didn't get to tell a
story. I didn't get to pass out the snack.
I didn't find anything for Miss Cherry. And . . ."
"And what, my girl?" Grandpa asked.

How could Iris tell Grandpa that she didn't
want him to be the teacher anymore?
She just wanted him to be Grandpa.

"Iris, is it hard having me be your teacher?"
asked Grandpa.

"Really hard," said Iris.

"I understand, but school is almost over,"
said Grandpa.

4. Ice Cream

On the way home from school, Grandpa said,
"This was not an easy day, was it?"

"No," said Iris.

"But we got through it," said Grandpa.

"I think we should celebrate."

"Oh yes!" said Iris.

Iris and Grandpa went to
the Rainbow Café.
They sat on their favorite stools.
They ordered their favorite ice cream.

Iris had a vanilla ice-cream sundae with
chocolate syrup and whipped cream.
Grandpa had a strawberry ice-cream cone.

"Delicious," said Iris.

"Superb," said Grandpa.

They ate every last bite.

On the way home, Iris found
just the right present
for Miss Cherry.

The next morning,

Iris could not wait for the day to begin.

Miss Cherry was back.

Walter was waiting.

And, best of all,

Grandpa was her grandpa again.